UNCLE WIGGILY AND HIS FRIENDS

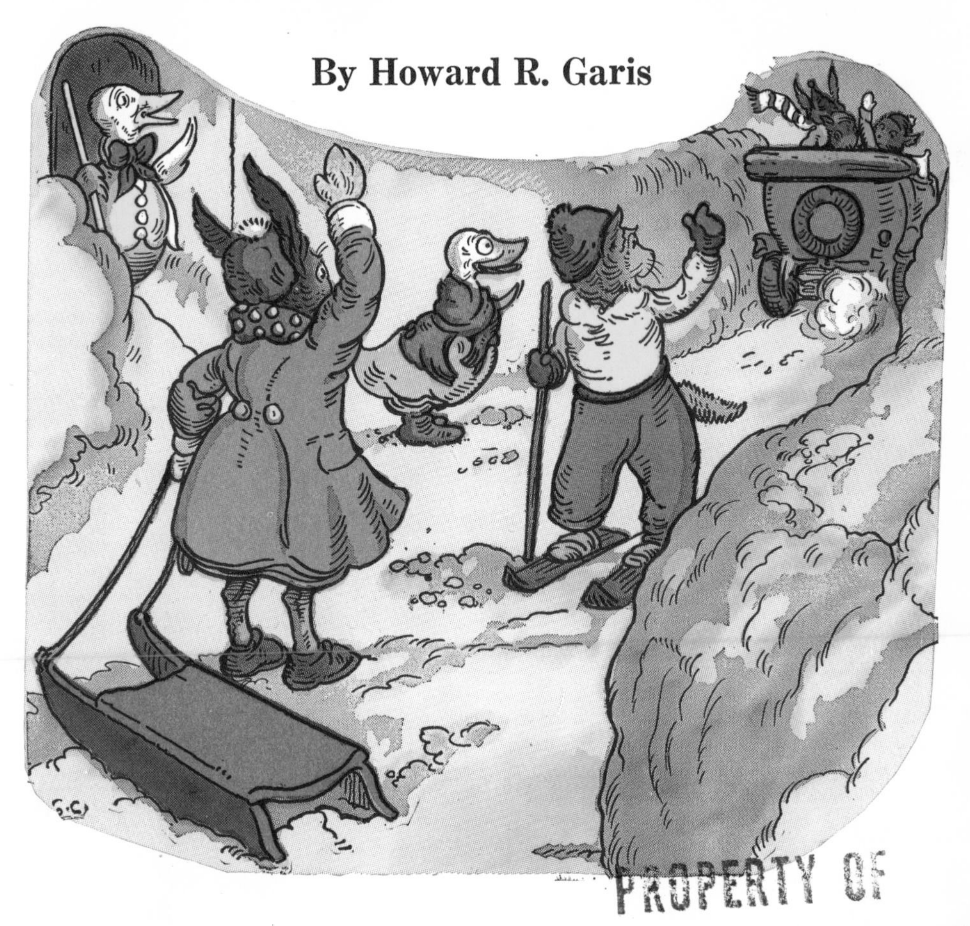

By Howard R. Garis

PLATT & MUNK, *Publishers*
NEW YORK
A Division of Grosset & Dunlap

ISBN 0-448-40504-0 (Trade Edition)
ISBN 0-448-13023-8 (Library Edition)

UNCLE WIGGILY AND THE BARBER

By HOWARD R. GARIS

One day Uncle Wiggily Longears started out for a ride in his automobile. It had a turnip steering wheel that he could nibble on when he was hungry.

Nurse Jane Fuzzy Wuzzy, the muskrat lady housekeeper asked: "Why are you taking your rheumatism crutch along, Uncle Wiggily? You won't need it when you are in the automobile."

"Oh, you never can tell," answered the rabbit gentleman. "I might want to get out and walk for a while."

So away went Uncle Wiggily in his auto, with the red, white and blue striped crutch, like a barber's pole, on the seat beside him. The rabbit gentleman rode on and on, and pretty soon he came to a place where there was a little shop, made from corn-cobs. In front of the corn-cob shop

was a nice monkey barber gentleman, and a little poodle dog. The little poodle dog was singing this happy song:

"Barber, barber, shave a pig,
How many hairs will make a wig?
Four and twenty—that's enough,
Give the barber a pinch of snuff."

"Very good! Very good!" cried the barber monkey, as he came out of his shop. He was wearing a white apron, and carrying a pair of scissors in one paw and a shaving mug, full of white, soapy lather in the other. "Very good, little poodle dog!" exclaimed the barber monkey. "But where is my pinch of snuff?"

"Here," answered the dog, giving it to the barber monkey. Then the monkey sneezed three times, and right after that he cut the little poodle dog's hair. He made a fluffy tuft on the end of his tail, and ruffles on his legs and a lot of fluffy hair around the doggie's neck, until he looked just like the lion in the circus.

"There you are, doggie," said the barber monkey. "Now, you have a nice hair-cut. Twenty-five barks, if you please."

"Oh, my mamma will pay you!" cried the little doggie as he did a somersault in the air. And before the barber

monkey could stop him, that mischievous little poodle pulled up the barber's pole and away he ran down the street with it, just like Tom, the piper's son.

"Here, come back with my pole if you please!" cried the monkey barber. "If I don't have a red, white and blue pole out in front of my place, no one will know this is a barber shop! Come back, I beg of you!"

But the poodle doggie only ran on the faster, and soon he was out of sight.

"That's too bad!" exclaimed Uncle Wiggily, who had seen what the poodle dog did. "Shall I chase after him in my auto, and bring back your barber pole?"

"No, thank you," said the barber monkey. "That little doggie is not bad. But unless I have the pole out in front of my shop the pig will not know the place when he comes marching by, and I can't shave him and make a wig."

"Say no more!" cried Uncle Wiggily in a jolly voice. "I have the very thing for you. I will let you take my red, white and blue striped barber pole crutch. You can put that in front of your shop until the poodle dog brings back the one he took."

"Thank you kindly," said the barber monkey. Then he stuck Uncle Wiggily's crutch up in front of the shop. It looked so like a real pole that when the pig, who wanted to be shaved came past, he knew at once where to go.

"You have been very good to me, Uncle Wiggily," said

the barber monkey, as he began to shave the pig. "Some day I will be kind to you."

That afternoon the old rabbit gentleman was out walking. He came to a place where some raccoon gentlemen were putting a new roof on their hollow stump house. The raccoons had a big kettle full of warm, black tar. They would spread this out thin, and then sprinkle little white gravel stones on top of the tar to make a new roof.

"Ha! This is very interesting," exclaimed Uncle Wiggily. "I must look into this," and he jumped on the edge of the kettle of warm, melted tar. All of a sudden his paws slipped and right into the sticky black tar he fell!

"Ouch! Oh, dear! This is terrible. Help! Help!" cried Uncle Wiggily. Luckily he had not fallen in head first so he could call for help.

"Quick!" cried the biggest raccoon. "We must help Uncle Wiggily out of the tar!"

Then, with their sticks, they lifted poor Uncle Wiggily out of the tar-kettle. Oh! but he was a dreadful sight. He was as black as a lump of coal and as sticky as the cork of a molasses jug.

"Quick! Send for Dr. Possum!" he called. But before they could do that something else happened.

Along the street came Jimmie Wibblewobble, the boy duck, with a bagful of geese feathers over his back. He was taking them to Mrs. Bushytail, who was to make them into a sofa pillow.

When Jimmie saw Uncle Wiggily all covered with tar, the little boy duck was so surprised that he dropped the bag of feathers.

In an instant the wind blew the bag open and scattered the feathers, and what is worse, the wind blew them all over Uncle Wiggily. On the warm, sticky, black tar the feathers blew. There they stuck, so that Uncle Wiggily looked like a chicken turned upside down.

"Oh, dear" cried the rabbit gentleman. "This is terrible."

"Oh, what shall I ever do to look like myself?" asked Uncle Wiggily.

"Ha! I can soon fix you!" exclaimed a voice, and there stood the barber monkey with his scissors, and his shaving mug of white, soapy lather.

"I will shave the tar and feathers off you, Uncle Wiggily," said the barber. "You were so kind to lend me your crutch for my pole, that I want to be kind to you."

"Then please shave me!" cried the rabbit gentleman. The monkey barber carefully lathered Uncle Wiggily, and shaved off the tar and feathers as nicely as you please.

When he had finished, Uncle Wiggily was just like himself, only his fur was a little shorter. But that did not matter, as it would soon grow out again.

So that's how the kind barber monkey shaved Uncle Wiggily, and the rabbit gentleman never looked into a tar-kettle again. Soon the little poodle doggie brought back the monkey barber's pole, and everybody was happy again. And next I will tell you about Uncle Wiggily and The Apple Dumpling.

UNCLE WIGGILY AND THE BARBER

Uncle Wiggily from head to toe
Was tarred and feathered, we all know
But, Barber Monkey down the street
Has made him, once again, look neat.
His colored crutch, red, white, and blue
Makes Barber Pole that's very new.

UNCLE WIGGILY AND THE APPLE DUMPLING

By HOWARD R. GARIS

Nurse Jane Fuzzy Wuzzy, the kind muskrat lady, who lived with Uncle Wiggily Longears, was in the kitchen clattering away with the pots and pans and kettles. All the while she was singing away like this:

"Merrily today I bake,
Perhaps 'twill be a chocolate cake,
Or e'en a pudding—who can tell?
Uncle Wiggily likes them well,
Puddings, pies—I both can bake;
Now, let's see; what shall I make?"

"Well, my goodness me, sakes alive and some chocolate drops!" exclaimed Uncle Wiggily. "Nurse Jane is certainly good to me."

"What are you making that smells so good, Nurse Jane?"

"An apple dumpling," said she.

"They are not made with turnips, are they?" asked Uncle Wiggily.

"The very idea! Certainly not!" cried Nurse Jane. "They are made of apples and sugar and flour and water and cinnamon, and spice and everything nice."

"Good!" cried Uncle Wiggily.

"Oh, mercy me!" exclaimed Nurse Jane, suddenly jumping up.

"What's the matter?" asked Uncle Wiggily.

"I thought I smelled the apple dumplings burning. No, they're all right," she said, as she lifted from the oven two of the nicest apple dumplings you could ever imagine.

"What!" cried Uncle Wiggily. "Two apple dumplings! Indeed this is a lucky day for me! That is fine!"

"Oh, please don't be so hasty," begged Nurse Jane, as she poured the cabbage sauce over the dumplings. "Only one is for you, Uncle Wiggily. I made the other for Grandfather Goosey Gander. I'll put it in a pail, and cover it

up, so it will keep hot a long time. Then you may take it to him in your automobile."

"I'll do so at once!" said Uncle Wiggily. "And when I come back I'll eat my apple dumpling. Oh, what a lovely day it is!"

Nurse Jane placed one of the apple dumplings in a pail, where it could cuddle up all by itself and keep hot. A little later Uncle Wiggily drove his automobile around to the front door. Into the machine he got, and, with the pail under a blanket, away he started over the hills and through the woods, to Grandfather Goosey Gander's.

The old gentleman rabbit had not gone very far before he came to a lonesome part of the woods. He was hurrying through it as fast as he could go, for he thought maybe some bad dogs might be there, and chase him. All at once, he came to a little stump house.

It was a house made in a hollow stump, a very poor and shabby sort of a house. The windows were stuffed with bits of rags and papers, instead of having glass in them. The door hung by only one hinge, and there was no smoke coming out of the chimney.

"Some poor animals must live in there," said Uncle Wiggily to himself. "I wonder if I could help them?"

Then he heard, from the hollow stump house, a sad little voice, crying:

"Oh, mamma, I'm so cold and hungry!"

And another little voice said:

"Oh, mamma, if I could only get warm, and have something nice to eat. Even a crust of nut-bread would do."

"Ha!" exclaimed Uncle Wiggily Longears, the rabbit gentleman, blinking his eyes. "This is where I must do something."

He got softly out of his automobile, and went to one of the broken windows of the stump house. He looked in, and he saw a poor old squirrel lady, and her two little squirrel children. And, oh! how hungry they looked. And how cold!

"Ha! I'll soon fix this!" cried Ungle Wiggily. Back to his auto he went so fast that he hardly needed his rheumatism barber pole crutch. He caught up the pail with the hot apple dumpling in it, and into the stump house he went on the jump.

"Here, little squirrels, he cried—"here is something to make you warm. Just gather around it, and toast your tootsies! I'll soon have a regular fire here, and you'll be all right, but get warm at this pail first."

And the squirrel mamma, and the little cold squirrel children, did so, looking at Uncle Wiggily with strange eyes, as if they thought he was a fairy and might vanish up the chimney, taking the nice pail with him.

He took the cover off the pail, and what a delicious smell came out from the apple dumpling.

"There you are!" cried the old rabbit gentleman. "Eat all you like. It can't hurt you!"

And I wish you could have seen those squirrel children and their mamma eat!

And while the poor squirrels were eating the dumpling, Uncle Wiggily went to the store in his auto. He bought

coal for the stove and lots of things for the squirrel family to eat, so they were never cold and hungry again. Then Uncle Wiggily went home.

"Where's that other apple dumpling?" he asked Nurse Jane. "I want to take it to Grandfather Goosey."

"Why!" cried the muskrat lady. "I gave it to you! Did you lose it?"

"Never mind what happened to it!" laughed Uncle Wiggily. "I'll just take this one to him, and you can make me another," and off he went with the second apple dumpling. This one he really took to Grandpa Goosey.

And, if the loaf of bread doesn't get a toothache and jump out of the oven into the dishpan I'll tell you about Uncle Wiggily Learns to Dance.

UNCLE WIGGILY AND THE APPLE DUMPLING

An apple dumpling very hot
Is what these squirrels would like a lot,
And Uncle Wiggily with this dish
Is bringing true that special wish.
It tastes so good they just can't wait
They want to taste what's on the plate.

UNCLE WIGGILY LEARNS TO DANCE

By HOWARD R. GARIS

One day Uncle Wiggily saw Sammie and Susie, the rabbit boy and girl, walking along with bags in their paws.

"Where are you going?" asked Uncle Wiggily. "You seem as if you were going after chestnuts, or maybe after carrots, but that cannot be as it is now winter."

"No, we are not going after any of those things, Uncle Wiggily," answered Susie. "We are going to take our dancing lesson. Wouldn't you like to come?"

"What! Me go to dancing class?" exclaimed Uncle Wiggily. "I am much too old for that—too old and stiff. Besides you forget I have the rheumatism."

"Dancing might be good for it" suggested Sammie. "It might limber you up. See, we have our dancing slippers in

these bags. Come to our dancing school if you like. There are many older animals there than you are."

"No, I think I had better not," said Uncle Wiggily.

So Sammie and Susie went to dancing class, where they learned to hop and glide about on top of a flat stump.

Uncle Wiggily went on his way, and the farther he went the more he thought about dancing. He remembered how very glad and happy every one seemed who danced.

"I wonder if I could dance?" thought Uncle Wiggily. "No one can see me if I am awkward and stiff. I'll just try a few steps."

So he did, hopping about with his rheumatism crutch. But as soon as he started to do a waltz, he cried out:

"Ouch! Oh, my! Oh, dear!"

"What is the matter?" asked a voice close beside him, and looking around, Uncle Wiggily saw a little brown and white mousie lady.

"Oh, excuse me if I frightened you," he said, "but I just tried to dance and my rheumatism hurt me so I had to cry out. I will go away, dancing was not made for old rabbit gentlemen."

And then, before he could move, Uncle Wiggily saw the

nice little brown and white mousie lady begin waltzing about on top of a flat stump.

Around and around she went, whirling about on the tips of her hind paws, and very lightly and prettily too.

"Ha!" cried Uncle Wiggily, surprised-like. "You are quite a dancer. How did you learn to do it?"

"Why, it comes natural in our family," said the mousie. "I am one of the waltzing mice. If you like, I will teach you to dance."

"Good!" cried Uncle Wiggily. "That will be fine. I can come out here in the woods, where no one can laugh at me for being stiff, and I can learn to dance. Then I can surprise Sammie and Susie, and Nurse Jane Fuzzy Wuzzy."

"Then I'll give you the first lesson," said the mousie lady, as she waltzed around again on her hind paws.

Every day after that Uncle Wiggily slipped quietly off to the woods to take a dancing lesson from the mouse. At

first it was hard work, but soon he was not so stiff, and his rheumatism did not pain him so, and by and by he was a good dancer.

He learned to do the rabbit crawl, and the bunny jump as well as the cheese nibble and the cracker snap.

One day, when Uncle Wiggily had been taking dancing lessons for some time, Nurse Jane Fuzzy Wuzzy said:

"Where do you go, off by yourself, every day, Uncle Wiggily?"

"Oh," he said laughing, "Some day I will tell you."

"Oh, tell me now!" teased Nurse Jane, but Uncle Wiggily would not. And he kept on taking dancing lessons.

One day Nurse Jane said to him:

"Uncle Wiggily, Sammie and Susie are going to have a little party. They have invited us. Shall we go?"

"Why, yes, of course!" exclaimed the rabbit gentleman.

"The only trouble is," went on Nurse Jane, "that there is going to be dancing, and you know you——

"Oh, I dare say I can sit and look on with you," interrupted the rabbit gentleman, sort of blinking his eyes.

"Very well," said Nurse Jane.

So she and Uncle Wiggily got ready to go to the party Uncle Wiggily dressed himself in his best suit, and Nurse Jane had on a sky-blue dress with pink trimmings.

All the animal children were at the party, and when the musician canary birds began to play and sing all the young folks began to dance.

Johnnie and Billie Bushytail, the squirrels, did a fine chestnut glide with Jennie Chipmunk and Susie Littletail; and Charlie and Arabella, the chicken children, did an omelet skip that was as fine as anything ever seen.

Louder and faster played the canary bird music. Uncle Wiggily kept time by tapping his crutch on the floor. He looked at Nurse Jane in her blue dress, and noticed that she was tapping her paw on the side of her chair.

"Do you like to dance, Nurse Jane?" he asked.

"Very much," she answered. "I used to be a fine dancer when I was young. But I have no one here to dance with."

"I will dance with you!" cried Uncle Wiggily, suddenly.

"What you? Can you dance?" asked Nurse Jane, surprised-like.

"I certainly can!" cried Uncle Wiggily.

"Won't you step on my dress and tear it?" asked Nurse Jane, anxiously. "Or tread on my toes?"

"Try me!" laughed Uncle Wiggily. So he laid aside his crutch, and while the birds made louder and still faster music, Uncle Wiggily led Nurse Jane out to the middle of the floor, and there he danced with her.

"Oh, how well you dance!" cried Miss Fuzzy Wuzzy.

"How did you manage it? I never knew you could do it!"

Then Uncle Wiggily told about taking private lessons in the woods from the mouse lady, and Nurse Jane laughed and said:

"Well, you certainly can keep a secret!"

Then she and Uncle Wiggily danced the apple dumpling turnover, and the strawberry shortcake trot, and every one of the animal children clapped their paws and said it was fine. Then the party went on, and Uncle Wiggily danced and danced and his rheumatism did not hurt him a bit.

And in the next story, if the moving picture doesn't run so fast that it jumps out of the window and scares our cat, so she falls into the milk bottle, I'll tell you about Uncle Wiggily and the Snow Plow.

UNCLE WIGGILY LEARNS TO DANCE

Waltzing mouse is having fun,
Showing how it should be done.
Cricket plays so merrily
Watching Uncle Wiggily.
Dancing lessons every day
Keeps them feeling young and gay.

George
Carlson

UNCLE WIGGILY AND THE SNOW PLOW

By HOWARD R. GARIS

"There, I knew it would happen!" exclaimed Nurse Jane Fuzzy Wuzzy one morning, as she looked out of the window of the hollow stump bungalow.

"What has happened?" asked Uncle Wiggily as he came downstairs to breakfast. "Have you broken something, Nurse Jane?"

"No, indeed, I haven't broken anything," said she. "But I knew that cold March wind would bring snow — now it has. See, it is snowing hard."

"Hum! So it is!" said Uncle Wiggily. "I guess I had better not go out in this storm."

"And I guess the same thing!" cried Nurse Jane. "I would not let you go out on a day like this."

"So all Uncle Wiggily could do was to sit by the window

and watch the snow flakes sift down and the wind pile it in big drifts. It looked as if Mother Goose was shaking her feather beds.

It was no more fun for Uncle Wiggily to stay in the house all day, than it is for you boys and girls.

"I wish it would stop snowing!" Uncle Wiggily said, over and over again. "I do so want to see Grandfather Goosey Gander. I have not been over in a long while to play Scotch checkers with him. The last time I started a big wind blew me away, and I haven't had a chance to call on him since."

And it did not seem as if he were going to get a chance now, for the snow was falling faster and thicker.

"I declare, no one is out at all," went on the rabbit gentleman, when he had sat by his window for some time. He had not even seen Sammie Littletail, the rabbit boy, hopping past. It had to be a very hard storm indeed to keep Sammie in let me tell you.

"No one would go out today who did not have to," said Nurse Jane. "We are all better off in the house when it storms like this."

As there was nothing else to do, Uncle Wiggily stayed in all day, and he didn't have a chance to see any of his friends. At night he went to bed and in the morning when he got up, the snow had stopped falling.

But, oh! How deep it was! All around the hollow stump bungalow the snow was piled, so high that it was almost over Uncle Wiggily's head. It was banked up on the door steps and window sills, and when Nurse Jane opened the front door a lot of snow came in the house.

"Oh, this is too bad!" she exclaimed. "Now we can't get out to buy anything from the store. We are snowed in!"

"Ha! So we are!" cried Uncle Wiggily. "Ha! Ha!"

"Well, I don't call it anything to laugh at," said Nurse Jane. "It is far from being funny."

"I was not laughing because we are snowed in," went on

the rabbit gentleman. "I laughed because I just happened to think of a way to get out and go to the store, and also visit my friends who must all be snowed in. I'm going to help them to get out."

"How," asked Nurse Jane.

"I'll soon show you," answered the rabbit gentleman, as he went to the cellar, where he had put his automobile.

Soon Uncle Wiggily was hammering away down in the cellar. He sawed and pounded, and whistled loudly as he always did when he was happy.

"I wonder what he can be making?" thought Nurse Jane.

She quickly found out, for soon she heard a funny noise at the back door. When she looked out she saw Uncle Wiggily's automobile standing in the snow. He had run it right up the cellar steps. And the funny part of it was that in front of the automobile were fastened some boards, coming to a sharp point. The sharp point of boards pointed out ahead of the auto, like the cow-catcher on a choo-choo locomotive.

"What in the world is that?" cried Nurse Jane.

"That is my automobile snow plow," answered Uncle Wiggily. "I have put a sharp plow out in front of my auto, and when I start the machine the plow will push the snow away.

"Then I can open paths all around here, and my friends

can walk out without getting into a deep drift. Then you can go to the stores without having to wear rubber boots."

"That will be very nice—if you can do it," said Nurse Jane.

"You watch and see me do it!" Uncle Wiggily said.

So he got into his auto, and turned on the gasoline and he moved the what-you-may-call-it over one way, and the thing-a-ma-bob over the other way. Then he pulled on some handles and, presto-chango! off went the auto.

And, as it moved along the snow was tossed off to one side or the other, leaving a nice smooth path behind.

Through the big drifts the rabbit gentleman drove the auto snow plow, scattering the snow right and left, and opening up broad paths. First he made a path to Grandfather Goosey Gander's house. Then to Sammie Littletail's.

Then to the home of Alice, Lulu and Jimmie Wibblewobble, the ducks and then to the coop where Charlie and Arabella Chick lived.

"Oh joy! Here is Uncle Wiggily! He has made paths for us, and now we can get out and play!" cried all the animal children. They were very happy because they had been snowed in too.

All around animal town Uncle Wiggily drove his auto snow plow, scattering the big drifts. Soon he had all the paths cleared.

Then he went over to play Scotch checkers with Grandpa Goosey Gander and, when it was time to go home the rabbit gentleman could ride in his auto without any plow on it.

And that's all for a while. But in the next story if the pancake-turner doesn't go to a dance with the egg-beater and break its handle, I'll tell you about Uncle Wiggily and The Wagon Sleds.

UNCLE WIGGILY
AND THE SNOW PLOW

Just what is this built out in front?
It is quite a clever stunt.
With auto snow plow all in one,
Clearing roads is swiftly done.
Soon the children laugh and play
'Cause Uncle Wiggily cleared the way.

George
Carlson

UNCLE WIGGILY AND THE WAGON SLEDS

By HOWARD R. GARIS

One day, when Uncle Wiggily, the nice old rabbit gentleman, was out taking a walk, he came to the house where Jackie and Peetie Bow Wow, the puppy dog boys lived.

"I think I will go in and see Peetie and Jackie," said Uncle Wiggily to himself. "I have not called on them in some time, and a little rest will do me good after my walk."

Into the doggie's house went the rabbit gentleman, but when he got there he saw a strange sight. For, off in one corner sat Peetie, and oh! what a scowly-owly look was on Peetie's face. And in another corner was Jackie Bow Wow, and on his face was an even worse scowly-owly look.

"Why, whatever is the matter?" asked Uncle Wiggily in surprise. "Have you boys the toothache?"

"No, they have not," said Mrs. Bow Wow coming in from

the kitchen, where she was baking some dog biscuits and puppy cakes. "No, Uncle Wiggily, I am sorry to say that Jackie and Peetie are rather naughty."

"Naughty—you amaze me!" exclaimed the rabbit gentleman. "Why, what has happened?"

"It's all on account of the weather," went on Mrs. Bow Wow. As for Jackie and Peetie they didn't even speak to Uncle Wiggily, and they were so fond of him. But it was just because they were cross and unpleasant; that's all. They weren't their real selves, you see.

"On account of the weather, eh?" went on Uncle Wiggily. "Why I don't see anything the matter with it. The sun is shining, there is no snow, and———"

"That's just the trouble!" burst out Jackie. "There is no snow, and we want to go coasting with our sleds, and we can't go!"

"It's—it's just—mean–that's what it is!" said Peetie, very crossly.

"Hoity-toity!" cried Uncle Wiggily, "So you boys think

the weather man has made all this trouble? Why can't you do something else besides sliding down hill?"

"We don't want to," said Peetie. "We want to play with our sleds but we can't slide down on bare ground; can we, Uncle Wiggily?"

"No, I suppose not," said the rabbit gentleman, slowly. "But how would you like to come for a ride in my automobile? That can go whether there is any snow on the ground or not. Come along and we may have an adventure."

"No!" said Peetie.

"No!" said Jackie, and they both looked very cross and unpleasant. I guess they were unhappy, and maybe a bit sorry. Sometimes, you see, when you get in the way of being naughty, it's hard to get back into the way of being good again.

I don't mean you, exactly, but perhaps you've seen some one who was that way—like Peetie and Jackie.

"Hum! Well!" said Uncle Wiggily. He did not know just what to make of this for they had never acted so before.

Then the old rabbit gentleman had a new idea. There

came a twinkle into his red eyes, and even his nose blinkled and twinkled, and he said:

"Well, boys, if I could fix it so you could slide down hill on your sleds, even if there is no snow on the ground, would you like that?"

"Yes, we would," said Jackie, and he smiled the least little bit, but not much.

"Only it can't be done," said Peetie.

"Well," said Uncle Wiggily, slowly, "I'm not saying that it is an easy thing to make a sled that will go down hill on the bare ground. But I can try it."

"Just see how kind your Uncle Wiggily is to you," said Mrs. Bow Wow. "Aren't you sorry you were naughty?"

"Yes, I guess so," spoke Jackie. "But I'd like to see that new sled, first."

"Well, I'll go out in your barn and make it," said the rabbit gentleman. "Where are your sleds?"

"Here!" cried Jackie and Peetie eagerly, as they brought them to Uncle Wiggily.

"Well, now you stay here until you hear me whistle,"

spoke the rabbit gentleman, "and by that time the sleds will be ready for you and you can ride down hill, even if there is no snow."

Uncle Wiggily went out to the barn, and what do you think he did? Why he took some wheels off the two old baby-dog carriages he found out there. He fastened four wheels to Peetie's sled and four wheels to Jackie's. And when you sat on the sleds you could roll down a hill as nicely as in an automobile. You could easily pretend it was winter, and there was snow on the ground, for there were the sleds, runners and everything.

Uncle Wiggily whistled, and out came running Jackie and Peetie Bow Wow. They saw the wagon sleds Uncle Wiggily had made for them, and they said:

"Oh, thank you so much!" and they didn't scowl any more.

I guess they were sorry for having been cross, just because there was no snow.

"Now, for a good coast!" cried Peetie.

"Hurray!" cried Jackie.

Not far away was a little hill, and soon the two puppy dog

boys were riding down this on their wagon sleds, that had baby-dog carriage wheels nailed to them. Oh, what fun they had!

Then along came Sammie Littletail, the rabbit boy, and Jimmie Wibblewobble, the duck boy, and many other animal children. When they saw the wagon sleds Uncle Wiggily had made they all said:

"Oh!" just like that.

Peetie and Jackie let their friends take turns on the new wagon sleds, that were good even if there was no snow. All the boy animals said they were going to make some sleds of their own next day. And I guess they did.

And if the penwiper doesn't go out on the front stoop and pretend that it's the doormat to fool the letter man, I'll tell you about Uncle Wiggily and The Peppermint.

UNCLE WIGGILY AND THE SLEDS

Sometimes sleds can whiz and go
When there isn't any snow.
Put two wheels on either side
And you still can have a slide.
That is what these doggies do,
Perhaps you can try it, too.

Notice
I have gone
to a baseball-
moving-picture
show.
Mr. Monkey-Doodle

UNCLE WIGGILY AND THE PEPPERMINT

By HOWARD R. GARIS

"Uncle Wiggily, would you mind going to the store for me?" asked Nurse Jane Fuzzy Wuzzy, the muskrat lady housekeeper, one morning, as she came in from the kitchen of the hollow stump bungalow.

"Go to the store? Why of course I'll go, Miss Fuzzy Wuzzy" answered the bunny uncle. "Which store?"

"The Drug Store."

"The drug store? What do you want; talcum powder or court plaster?"

"Neither one," answered Nurse Jane. "I want some peppermint."

"Peppermint candy?" asked Uncle Wiggily.

"Not exactly" went on Nurse Jane. "But I want a little of the peppermint juice with which some kind of candy is flavored. I want to take some peppermint juice my-

self, for I have indigestion. Dr. Possum says peppermint is good for it.

"I'll get you the peppermint with pleasure," said the bunny uncle, starting off with his tall silk hat and his red, white and blue striped rheumatism barber pole crutch.

"Better get it in a bottle," spoke Nurse Jane, with a laugh. "You can't carry peppermint in your pocket, unless it's peppermint candy, and I don't want that kind."

"All right," Uncle Wiggily said, and then, with the bottle, which Nurse Jane gave him, he hopped on, over the fields and through the woods to the drug store.

But when Uncle Wiggily reached the drug store it was closed. There was a sign in the door which said the monkey-doodle gentleman who kept the drug store had gone to a baseball-moving picture show.

"I wonder where I am going to get Nurse Jane's peppermint?" asked Uncle Wiggily of himself. "I'd better go see if Dr. Possum has any."

But while Uncle Wiggily was going on through the woods once more, he gave a sniff and a whiff, and all of a sudden, he smelled a peppermint smell.

The rabbit gentleman stood still, looking around and making his pink nose twinkle like a pair of roller skates. While he was doing this along came a cow lady.

"What are you doing here, Uncle Wiggily?" she asked.

Uncle Wiggily told her how he had gone to the drug store for peppermint for Nurse Jane, and how he had found the store closed.

"But I smell peppermint here in the woods," said Uncle Wiggily. "Can it be that the drug store monkey-doodle has left some here for me?"

"No, what you smell is—that," said the cow lady, pointing her horns toward some green plants growing near a little babbling brook of water. The plants had dark red stems that were square instead of round.

"It does smell like peppermint," said Uncle Wiggily, going closer and sniffing and snuffing.

"It is peppermint," said the cow lady. "That is the peppermint plant you see."

"Oh, now I remember," Uncle Wiggily exclaimed. "They squeeze the juice out of the leaves, and that's peppermint flavor for candy or for indigestion."

“Exactly,” spoke the cow lady, “and I’ll help you squeeze out some of this juice in the bottle for Nurse Jane.”

Then Uncle Wiggily and the cow lady pulled up some of the peppermint plants and squeezed out the juice between two clean, flat stones.

"My! But this is strong!" cried the bunny uncle, as he smelled of the bottle of peppermint. It was so sharp that it made tears come into his eyes. "I should think that would cure indigestion and everything else."

"Tell Nurse Jane to take only a little of it in water," said the cow lady. "It is very strong. So be careful of it."

"I will," promised Uncle Wiggily. "And thank you for getting the peppermint for me. I don't know what I would have done without you."

Then he hopped on through the woods to the hollow stump bungalow. He had not quite reached it when, all of a sudden, there was a rustling in the bushes. From behind a bramble bush jumped a big black bear. Not a nice good bear, like Beckie Stubtail, but a bear who cried:

"Ah, ha! Oh, ho! Here is some one whom I can bite and scratch! A nice tender rabbit chap! Ah, ha! Oh, ho!"

"Are—are you going to scratch and bite me?" asked Uncle Wiggily.

"I am," said the bear snappish like. "Get ready. Here I come!" and he started toward Uncle Wiggily, who was so frightened that he could not hop away.

"I am going to hug you too" said the bear.

"Well, this is, indeed, a sorry day for me," said Uncle Wiggily sadly. "Still, if you are going to hug, bite and scratch me, I suppose it can't be helped."

"Not the least in the world can it be helped," said the bear, cross-like and unpleasant.

"Well, if you are going to hug me I had better take this bottle out of my pocket, so when you squeeze me the glass won't break," Uncle Wiggily said. "Here, when you are through being so mean to me perhaps you will take this to Nurse Jane for her indigestion, but don't hug her"

"I won't," promised the bear, taking the bottle which Uncle Wiggily handed him. "What's in it?"

Before Uncle Wiggily could answer the bear opened the bottle, and, seeing something in it, cried:

"I guess I'll taste this. Maybe it's good to eat." Down

his big, red throat he poured the strong peppermint juice, and then—well, I guess you know what happened.

"Oh, wow! Oh, me! Oh, my! Wow! Ouch! Ouchie! Itchie!" roared the bear. "My throat is on fire! I must have some water!" And, dropping the bottle, away he ran to the spring, leaving Uncle Wiggily safe, and not hurt a bit.

Then the rabbit gentleman hurried back and squeezed out more peppermint juice for Nurse Jane, whose indigestion was soon cured. And as for the bear, he had a sore throat for a week and a day.

So this teaches us that peppermint is good for scaring bears, as well as for putting in candy. And if the snow man doesn't come in our house and sit by the gas stove until he melts into a puddle of molasses, I'll tell you next about Uncle Wiggily and The Red Spots.

UNCLE WIGGILY
AND THE PEPPERMINT

Poor Uncle Wiggily looks so sad
He can't get in, you see,
But, He will fill the bottle up
Yes, very easily.
For peppermint grows in the woods
Its juice is extra strong
Its taste would scare the bear away
If one should come along.

UNCLE WIGGILY AND THE RED SPOTS

By HOWARD R. GARIS

Uncle Wiggily Longears was hopping along through the woods one fine day, when he heard a little voice calling to him:

"Oh, Uncle Wiggily! Will you have a game of tag with me?"

At first the bunny uncle thought the voice might belong to a bad fox or a harum-scarum bear, but when he had peeked through the bushes he saw that it was Lulu Wibblewobble, the duck girl.

"Have a game of tag with you? Why, of course, I will!" laughed Uncle Wiggily. "That is, if you will kindly excuse my rheumatism, and my red, white and blue crutch."

"Of course, I'll excuse it, Uncle Wiggily," said Lulu. "Only please don't tag me with the end of your crutch, for it tickles me, and when I'm tickled I have to laugh, and when I laugh I can't play tag."

"I won't" said Uncle Wiggily with a laugh.

So the little duck girl and the rabbit gentleman played tag in the woods.

Sometimes Lulu was "it" and Uncle Wiggily would be tagged by the foot or wing of the duck girl.

"Now for a last tag!" cried Uncle Wiggily when it was getting late. "I'll tag you this time, Lulu, and then we must go home."

"All right," agreed Lulu, and she ran and flew so fast that Uncle Wiggily could not tag her. Finally when Uncle Wiggily almost had his paw on the duck girl she flew right over a bush, and before Uncle Wiggily could stop himself, he had run into the bush until he was half way through it.

But luckily, it was not a scratchy briar bush, so no great harm was done, except that Uncle Wiggily's fur was a bit ruffled up.

"I guess I can't tag you this time, Lulu" laughed the bunny uncle. "We'll give up the game now, and I'll be "it" next time we play."

"All right, Uncle Wiggily," said Lulu. "I'll meet you here in the woods at this time tomorrow and I'll bring Alice and Jimmie with me, and we'll play tag again and have lots of fun."

"Fine!" said the bunny uncle, as he squirmed his way out of the bush.

Then he went on to his hollow stump bungalow, and Lulu went on to her duck pen house to have her supper of corn meal.

As Uncle Wiggily was sitting down to his supper of carrot ice cream with lettuce sandwiches, Nurse Jane Fuzzy Wuzzy looked at him and exclaimed:

"Why, Wiggy! What's the matter with you?"

"Matter with me? Nothing. I feel just fine!" he said.

“Why, you’re all covered with red spots!” went on the muskrat lady. “You are breaking out with the measles. I must send for Dr. Possum at once.”

“Measles? Nonsense!” exclaimed Uncle Wiggily. “I can’t have measles again. I’ve had them once.”

"Well, you are certainly all covered with red spots, and red spots are always measles" said the muskrat lady.

"You must go to bed at once," said Nurse Jane," and when Dr. Possum comes he'll tell you what else to do."

Uncle Wiggily looked at himself in a glass to make sure.

"Well, I guess I have the measles all right," he said. "But I don't see how I can have them twice. This must be a different kind than I had before."

It was dark when Dr. Possum came, and when he saw the red spots on Uncle Wiggily, he said:

"Yes, I guess they are measles all right. Lots of the animal children are down with them. But don't worry. Keep warm and quiet, and you'll be all right in a few days."

So Uncle Wiggily went to bed, red spots and all. Nurse Jane made him hot carrot and sassafras tea, with whipped cream and chocolate in it.

All the next day the bunny uncle stayed in bed with his red spots. He wanted very much to go out in the woods looking for an adventure.

When evening came and Nurse Jane was sitting out on the front porch of the hollow stump bungalow, she suddenly heard a quacking sound.

Coming up the path were Lulu, Alice and Jimmie Wibblewobble, the duck children.

"Where is Uncle Wiggily?" asked Lulu.

"He is in bed," answered Nurse Jane.

"Why is he in bed?" asked Jimmie. "Was he bad?"

"No, indeed," laughed Nurse Jane. "But your Uncle Wiggily is in bed because he has the red-spotted measles. What did you want of him?"

"He promised to meet us in the woods," answered Lulu, "and play tag with us. We waited and waited and played tag all by ourselves, even jumping in the bush, as Uncle Wiggily accidentally did when he was chasing me yesterday. So we came here to see what is the matter."

As the three duck children came up on the porch, where the bright light shone on them, Nurse Jane said:

"Oh, my goodness me! You ducks are all covered with red spots, too! You all have the measles! Oh, My!"

"Measles!" cried Jimmie, the boy duck, "Measles? These aren't measles, Nurse Jane! They are sticky, red berries from the bushes we jumped in as Uncle Wiggily did. The red berries are sticky, like burdock burrs. and they stuck to us."

"Oh, my goodness!" cried Nurse Jane. "Wait a minute, children!" Then she ran to where Uncle Wiggily was lying in bed. She leaned over and picked off some of the red spots from his fur.

"Why!" cried the muskrat lady. "You haven't the measles at all, Wiggy! It's just sticky, red berries in your fur, just as they are in the ducks' feathers. You're all right. Get up and have a good time!"

And Uncle Wiggily did and Nurse Jane combed the red, sticky burr-berries out of his fur. He didn't have the measles at all, for which he was very glad.

"My goodness! That certainly was a funny mistake for all of us," said Dr. Possum next day. "But the red spots surely did look like the measles." Which shows us that things are not always what they seem.

And if the lollypop doesn't take its sharp stick to make the baby carriage roll down the hill, I'll tell you the story of Uncle Wiggily and The Canoe.

UNCLE WIGGILY AND THE RED SPOTS

See the red and horrid spots!
Yes, there are just lots and lots.
Nurse is making quite a fuss,
Doctor looks so serious.
Here's the answer, if we look
At the story in the book.

George
Carlson

UNCLE WIGGILY AND THE CANOE

By HOWARD R. GARIS

"Hello, Sammie Littletail!" called a voice.

Sammie Littletail, the rabbit boy, sat up in his bed of green leaves, and listened carefully. He was camping on Candy Island in Sugar Lake, with Uncle Wiggily.

"Hello, Sammie Littletail!" called the voice again.

"And Uncle Wiggily, too!" shouted a second voice. "Hello to him also!"

The old gentleman rabbit, who was sleeping on another green, leafy bed near Sammie, opened his eyes.

"Is someone calling us?" he asked.

"It sounds like it, "replied Sammie, sort of sleepily.

Then two voices called together, "Where are you, Sammie? Come on out and have some fun!"

"Oh, I know who it is!" cried Sammie. "It is Johnnie and Billie Bushytail, the squirrel brothers!" And when Sammie looked out of the **large** tent, he saw the two squirrel boys frisking about on the ground, looking for nuts.

"We came to spend the day in camp with you, Sammie," explained Johnnie.

"And you are very welcome," said Uncle Wiggily, politely. "Nurse Jane Fuzzy Wuzzy, will you kindly get breakfast?"

Then the muskrat lady, who was also camping on the island, began to cook breakfast. The kind circus elephant got a pail of water in his trunk, at the well Uncle Wiggily had dug.

"Now, what shall we do to amuse Johnnie and Billie?" asked Uncle Wiggily after breakfast. "How would you all like to come for a ride in my airship?"

"Oh, fine!" cried Billie. "We came to the island in Grandfather Goosey Gander's steamboat, an airship ride, now, will be a nice change."

"Come along then," cried Uncle Wiggily, and soon they were sailing above the tree tops, and over Sugar Lake. They rode around and around in the airship, sitting on sofa cushions. After a while Sammie looking down, cried out:

"Oh, Uncle Wiggily! We are right over another island, different from ours. Let's see what's on it."

"All right" agreed the old gentleman rabbit, and down he sent his airship.

This island was not as large as the one on which Uncle Wiggily had made his camp. But still it was very nice. The old gentleman rabbit tied his airship to a tree, and then he and the rabbit boy and the squirrel brothers wandered about, looking for adventures.

They did not find one right away but they found some tame hickory nuts for the squirrels and some wild carrots

for the two rabbits, and every one had a good time. And then, before they knew it, they had an adventure.

As they walked back toward the place where they had left the airship, Sammie suddenly cried out:

"Why, its gone!"

"What's gone?" asked Uncle Wiggily, quickly.

"Your airship!" exclaimed Sammie. "Look, there it goes!" And, surely enough, there was the airship sailing back, all by itself, over the tree tops, toward Candy Island, where the camp was.

"Oh, dear!" cried Uncle Wiggily. "Come back here, airship! How are we ever to get off this island without the airship?"

But the airship did not answer, and it did not come back. On and on it sailed, all by itself, and soon it was out of sight.

"Oh, dear!" cried Uncle Wiggily. "I must have forgotten to turn off the electric fan, and while we were looking for an adventure the fan started up by itself and flew my airship away. Oh, what are we to do? We cannot swim back to Candy Island."

"Let's call for help," suggested Sammie. "Maybe the elephant or Nurse Jane will hear us. And, come to our rescue. Let's call as loud as we can."

So they shouted and yelled and called, separately and all

together, but it did no good. Neither Nurse Jane nor the elephant heard them, being too far away on Candy Island.

"Oh, we shall never get back home!" cried Billie and Johnnie Bushytail.

"We could if we had a boat," said Sammie bravely.

"That's it! A Boat!" cried Uncle Wiggily. "I should have thought of that before. There are some birch trees on this island. If we could strip off some of the bark we could make a bark canoe, just as the Indians used to do."

"Oh! we can strip off the bark for you," said the squirrel brothers. "We are used to doing that." So they peeled off long strips of bark with their sharp teeth.

Then Sammie and Uncle Wiggily sewed the strips together in the shape of a canoe, using long pieces of wild

grapevine for thread. They put sticky gum from the pine tree over the cracks, so no water would leak in. Soon they had a fine canoe.

"Now get in and we will go to our island," said Uncle Wiggily. But when they were in the canoe, which floated on the water, they could not move, for they had no oars or paddles to push themselves along.

"Oh, what shall we do?" cried Sammie.

"Ha! We will hoist our broad, bushy tails for sails!" cried the squirrel brothers. This they did. The wind blew on their tails, and away sailed the bark canoe, over the waters of the lake, on toward Candy Island. Soon they all arrived safely, and there, waiting for them, was the airship which had accidentally sailed away without them.

"But we didn't need it, as long as we had the bark canoe!" said Uncle Wiggily.

Nurse Jane and the elephant were very glad to see their friends safely back once more, and soon dinner was ready.

Now Boys and Girls, if you like Uncle Wiggily Stories ask your Mother or Daddy to get you a copy of UNCLE WIGGILY'S STORY BOOK. It has 36 more interesting adventures of Uncle Wiggily.

UNCLE WIGGILY AND THE CANOE

I wish I had a canoe
Like this birch bark one, do you?
Best of all, I like the sails
Made of furry squirrel tails.
Froggie, waving from the shore,
Wishes they had room for more.